A sleeping BEE-auty story...

Sleeping BEE-auty

BART'S BIG BOOK OF BEE

STORY BY
H.D. VESSER

ILLUSTRATED BY
ANA RANKOVIC

"OH!" said Bart; he had just been flying along when he BOUNCED.

Off a bee!

The bumblebee bounced off a bell, which was in a BIG blue field of bluebells.

Bizarre!

Bart couldn't believe his bedazzled eyes that were bulging at the bug.

"Bummer!" he said.

That bee was laying on a box in the barn ready for a battle.

But Bart, being behind the bee, burped.

He began to beg the bee for forgiveness for his bad behavior.

"Bee, please forgive me, I didn't mean to bump off of thee, believe me!"

"My name's Buzz Bee of the Queen's guard," said the bewildered bee.

"I am baffled at the bombardment of B's," said Buzz.

"I thought that was just how you spoke, dear Buzz Bee!" said Bart as he sat down by Buzz Bee, "dear me!"

"Ok, you and me, we'll stop with the B's."

"Ok, one two three!" said Bart.

"Hey... my name starts with B too. You can call me, Bart!"

"Then, we must be friends... definite B!" laughed the bee.

"Though this is an emergency!"

"My beautiful Queen Barb Bee!"

"Barb Bee is believed ...ah-hem..."

"I mean she is laying on the table, she's beloved to me!"

"She isn't moving! I don't know what to do."

"PLEASE! Help us," said Buzz, "I'll bee-long to you."

He pleaded and begged, "She is my little bee!" His little arms pumping so anxiously.

Bart wanted to help. But what could he do? He just didn't know. How could he help her? Exactly how so?

Bart took her hand and patted it
though, nothing would happen, and he felt
so low!

Buzz tried to wake her, again and again.
Barb Bee just lay there,

But suddenly then...

Zoe ran in, and she saw the bee. Buzz sitting sadly by his love, Barb Bee.

"Zoe," said Bart, "please, PLEASE, HELP ME!!

Zoe said, "Oh! I know how to help! I heard you both talking, you two silly B's."

"I've got a solution to solve it with ease."

"Oh, this ones in trouble!" said Bart, "Help us, PLEASE!"

Zoe was sucking on sweet tea she'd got,

She'd heard you have sugar; it helped bees a LOT!

"Quick!" she said, "I know just what to do,"

"Give her sugar water- she'll feel right as rain!"

"Scuse me; right now, let's stop this, her pain!"

Zoe sat by the bee, looked like she was gone,

But Zoe knew something- she would right this wrong!

"If I can get her to take one little sip, she looks like she's gone... but just give her a drip!"

She carefully poured tea on that sweet bee's tongue, and before she knew it, the spell was undone!

That bee started moving; she lapped up that nectar!

Buzz and his Barb Bee, they hugged from down under;

and smiling sweet, Zoe clapped her hands in wonder!

The wonder! The beauty! The love of it all!

Every act to save matters no matter how small.

To the honey bee on the Centennial trail: which lay motionless when I came across him while Rollerblading, I gave him a little of my sweet tea, and I continued on rollerblading. When I came back, he was moving, walking around, quite alive. That bee inspired this very story! Thank you, little guy!

To the letter B: to whom without I would not have this book! I got on a letter B kick one day, and just went with it...Isn't that when the best things happen?

To Dr. Seuss: who I grew up with and from whose books I first learned to read. "One Fish, Two Fish, Red Fish Blue Fish" was my first book as a child.

To Norina Cox Abelle: whos family who have helped their bee colony for generations with sugar water every year. (thank you for the advice on rationing of sugar water to save bees!)

To:

Pauline, Joe, Whitney, Jennie, Elaine, anyone who encouraged me in life to be creative.

And of course... the bat who came to breakfast.

H.Q. Vesser

Thanks to my Husband of 29 years, who spent many, many hours, months even, working with me and learning the things to organize and (re)publish all of our books in the best way possible. I have been amazed with what he has been able to do. Deeds, not words, are what really count in life, its the best kind of support. I LOVE YOU!!!

Thanks to Matthew Buza for all his excellent advice. He actually helped name this book. BRILLIANT!

Thank You to the Writers Cooperative Of The Pacific Northwest for their excellent advice.

Thank you to FinalStraw for allowing me to use their amazing straw in my book! www.finalstraw.com - Get your own rainbow straw, and check out their new product, Finalwipe!!!

YOU CAN SAVE BEE'S TOO! To save bees with sugar water:

Give them a ration of 50 water/50 sugar not cooked (stirred up) Help save a life! Pour under the bee carefully and then leave the bee. You may save a life! (Do not leave a pan out of it out for longer than a few hours, it can get rancid.)

H.D. Vesser lives in Washington State where she loves looking out the window at her desk watching the hummingbirds, birds, and nature writing about Bart. (Watch for the series!)

She loves going to book fairs to tell kids that "A blue butterfly touched my hair and turned it blue!" But it's really in memory of her friend Pauline and the butterfly she believes Pauline sent to tell her goodbye.

A. Rankovic, an illustrator from Belgrade Serbia does what she loves most... draws cartoony characters :)